This edition published by Parragon in 2010

Parragon
Queen Street House
4 Queen Street
Bath BA1 1HE, UK

ISBN 978-1-4454-0967-2

Printed in China

THE LITTLE MERMAID

Adapted by Amy Edgar

Bath • New York • Singapore • Hong Kong • Cologne • Delhi
Melbourne • Amsterdam • Johannesburg • Auckland • Shenzhen

Daydreams

Under the sea, merfolk hurried toward King Triton's palace. Everyone wanted a good seat for the concert.

The merfolk watched as Sebastian, the court composer, signaled for the music to begin. Six of King Triton's daughters sang and swirled around the stage to the sounds of the underwater orchestra.

Tonight King Triton's youngest daughter, Ariel, would sing her first solo. But when the giant clamshell opened, Ariel was nowhere to be seen.

"Ariel!" bellowed King Triton.

Nearby, Ariel had forgotten all about the concert. She and her friend Flounder were swimming around a sunken ship. Ariel loved looking for things from the human world above.

"It's wonderful!" she cried, finding a shiny fork.

"D-d-did you hear something?" asked Flounder.
"You're not getting cold fins, are you?" teased
Ariel.

Then Flounder spotted a large, dark shape
swimming right toward them! "Shark!" he yelled.

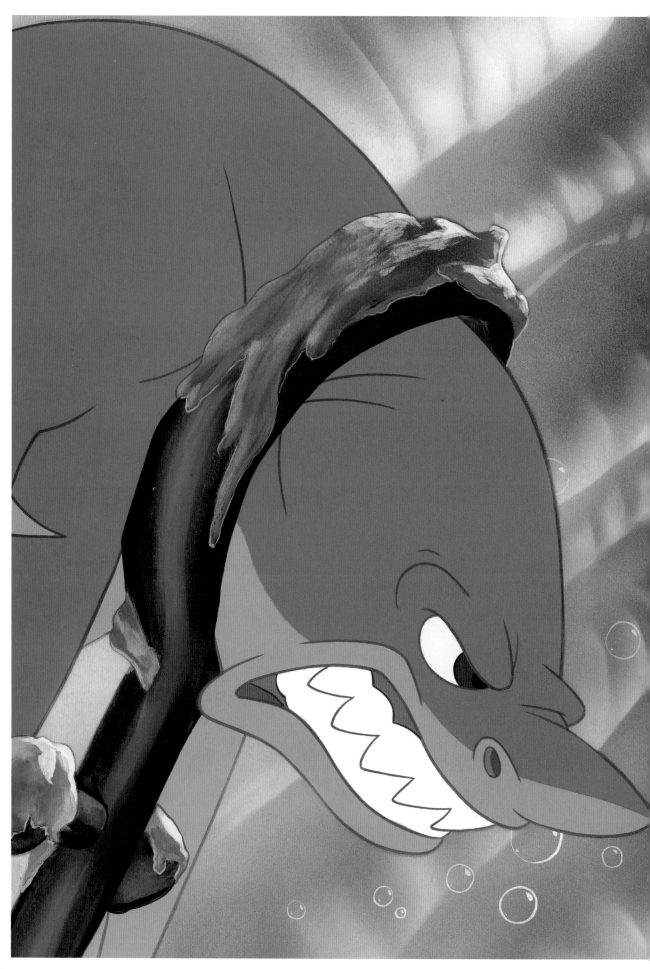

The two friends swam as fast as they could, but the shark could swim faster. So Ariel whisked Flounder through a small hole in an anchor. The hungry shark followed them and got stuck.

"Take that, you big bully!" Flounder jeered.

Ariel brought her new treasure to Scuttle, the seagull. "This is a dinglehopper," explained Scuttle, combing his feathers with the fork. "Humans use these to straighten their hair."

Deep below, the Sea Witch, Ursula, was gazing into her magic bubble, spying on Ariel.

Suddenly, Ariel remembered the concert! She hurried home to find King Triton waiting for her. He was angry about the ruined concert, but even angrier when he learned of Ariel's trip to the surface.

"Never go to the surface again!" he ordered.

Later, the King told Sebastian, "Ariel needs supervision, and you are just the crab to do it."

Meanwhile, Ariel was daydreaming in her secret grotto. "I don't see how a world that makes such wonderful things could be bad," she said.

The Prince

Ariel looked up and saw the shadow of a ship overhead. She swam to the surface to get a closer look. There, she saw a handsome young man. The other humans called him Prince Eric.

"Hurricane a-comin'!" a sailor shouted.

Howling wind tore at the ship's sails. Giant waves tossed it onto the jagged rocks. Prince Eric was thrown into the ocean!

Ariel frantically searched for the Prince. Finding him, she needed all her strength for the rescue.

Safe on the shore, Ariel sang to the unconscious Prince. At last, he began to awaken. "Someday, I'll be part of your world," she said, slipping into the sea.

Minutes later, the Prince's servant, Sir Grimsby, discovered him. "A girl rescued me," said the Prince groggily. "And she had the most beautiful voice."

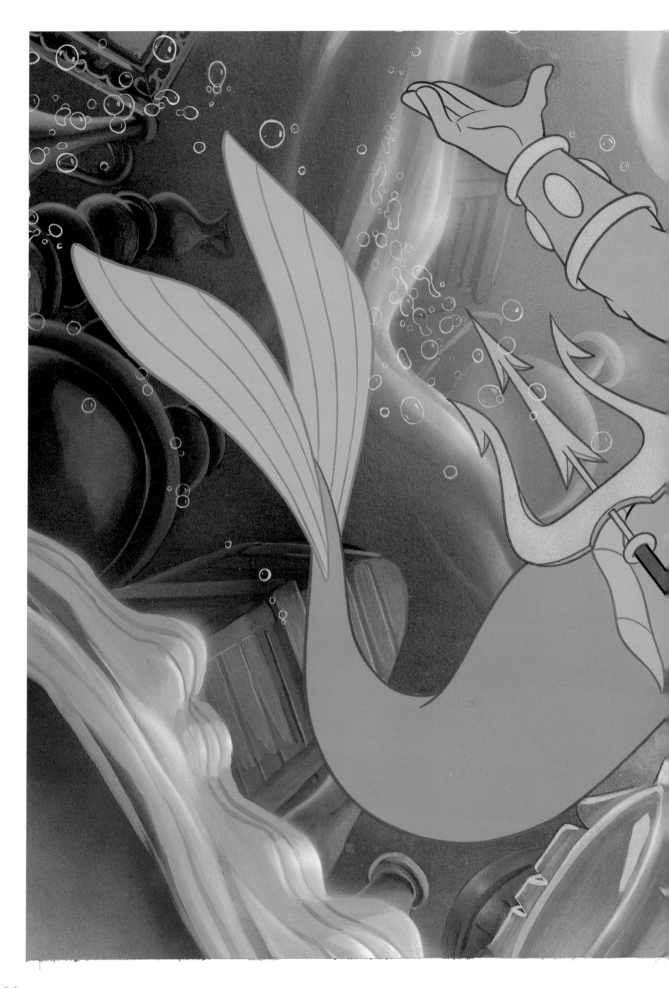

When King Triton found out that Ariel had been up to the surface again, he flew into a rage!

"Humans are all the same!" King Triton shouted. "Savage fish eaters, incapable of any feeling!" With a few strokes of his trident, he destroyed all of Ariel's treasures, and swam off.

Two sinister eels interrupted Ariel's sobbing. "We were sent by someone," they hissed, "who can make all your dreams come true."

The eels brought Ariel to Ursula. The Sea Witch was willing to help Ariel - in exchange for her voice!

"But," Ursula added, "the Prince must fall in love with you by sunset on the third day." If not, Ariel would change back into a mermaid and become Ursula's slave forever!

The ocean churned as Ariel's voice was captured inside a magical shell and her tail turned into legs.

Prince Eric and his dog, Max, found Ariel on the beach. "You seem very familiar to me," said Eric. "Have we met?" Ariel could only nod.

"Don't worry, I'll help you." He smiled. Although she looked like the girl who rescued him, Eric didn't think it could be her. She couldn't speak, much less sing!

That evening, Ariel appeared for dinner in a pretty gown. To the Prince's surprise, Ariel picked up her fork and began combing her hair, just as Scuttle had taught her!

Under the sea, a worried King Triton had not been able to find Ariel. "Leave no shell unturned until she's safe at home!" he told his servants.

Meanwhile, Ariel and Eric were happily rowing on a lagoon. Just as they were about to kiss, Ursula's eels overturned the boat!

That evening, the Prince heard someone singing. It was the voice of the girl who had saved him! Eric looked out to see Vanessa. He fell under her wicked spell.

When Ariel awoke the next morning, she saw Eric with Vanessa. "The wedding ship departs at sunset," the Prince told Grimsby.

Now Ariel had lost her chance at true love and was doomed to be Ursula's slave forever!

Aboard the wedding ship, Vanessa cackled, "Triton's daughter will be mine!"

Looking through the porthole, Scuttle saw the mirror reveal that Vanessa was really Ursula. He quickly found Ariel. "The Prince is marrying the Sea Witch in disguise!" he exclaimed.

51

"Find a way to stall that wedding!" Sebastian yelled to Scuttle as they took off to rescue Eric. Flounder helped Ariel along, but the sun was starting to set. There wasn't much time left!

Scuttle and his friends did their best to interrupt the wedding.

"Why you little . . ." Vanessa yelled, trying to defend herself.

In all the commotion, the magic shell shattered to the ground just as Ariel reached the ship.

"Eric?" spoke Ariel.

"You can talk!" said the Prince. "You're the one! It was you all the time."

Happy at last, the Prince leaned over to kiss Ariel.
But seconds before their lips met, the sun set.

"You're too late!" shouted Ursula, turning into her
beastly self. Ariel found her legs changed back into a
mermaid's tail.

"It's not you I'm after," Ursula told Ariel, whisking her into the sea. "I've got much bigger fish to fry." At those words, King Triton appeared.

Ursula told him about the deal she had made with Ariel. In return for his daughter's freedom, the King agreed to take Ariel's place as a slave.

"At last, this is mine," Ursula laughed, placing Triton's crown on her head. Using her new powers, Ursula grew to a monstrous size. "Now I am the ruler of all the ocean!"

But the brave Prince steered a ship over the raging waves right toward Ursula! The bow of the ship pierced her cold heart. Slowly, Ursula's horrendous body sank beneath the waves.

All at once, the ocean was calm and King Triton's power was restored. Now he realized how much Eric and Ariel loved each other. He changed Ariel's tail back into legs.

"I love you, Daddy," said Ariel, hugging him. He knew he would miss her terribly.

All the merfolk and sea creatures gathered to watch the happy couple's wedding. Everyone cheered as Eric kissed his new Princess. Then they sailed away to live happily ever after.

The End